Nate the Great
and the
Lost List

Nate the Great
and the
Lost List

by Marjorie Weinman Sharmat
and Marc Simont

A YEARLING BOOK

This is a work of fiction. Names, characters, places, and incidents either are the product of the authors' imagination or are used fictitiously. Any resemblance to actual persons, living or dead, events, or locales is entirely coincidental.

Library of Congress Cataloging-in-Publication Data is available upon request.

ISBN 978-0-440-46282-8 (pbk.) — ISBN 978-0-385-37677-8 (ebook)

Printed in the United States of America

68 67 66 65 64 63 62 61

For someone special,
my cousin Rhoda

I, Nate the Great,

am a busy detective.

One morning I was not busy.

I was on my vacation.

I was sitting under a tree

enjoying the breeze

with my dog, Sludge,

and a pancake.

He needed a vacation too.

My friend Claude

came into the yard.

I knew that he

had lost something.

Claude was always losing things.

"I lost my way to your house,"

he said. "And then I found it."

"What else did you lose?"

"I lost the grocery list

I was taking to the store.

Can you help me find it?"

"I, Nate the Great,

am on my vacation," I said.

"When will your vacation be over?"

"At lunch."

"I need the list before lunch,"
Claude said.

"Very well. I, Nate the Great,
will take your case.
Tell me, what was on the list?"

"If I could remember, I wouldn't
need the list," Claude said.

"Good thinking," I said.

"Does anyone know what
was on the list?"

"My father," Claude said.

"He wrote it."

"Good. Can you find your father?"

"No, he won't be home
until lunch."

"Can you remember
some of the list?"

"Yes," Claude said. "I remember
salt, milk, butter, flour,
sugar, and tuna fish."

"Now, tell me, where did you
lose the list?"

"If I knew, I could
find it," Claude said.

"You can't be sure
of that," I said.

"What streets did you walk on?"

"I'm not sure," Claude said.

"I lost my way a few times."

"Then I, Nate the Great,
know what to do.
I will draw a map
of every street
between your house
and the grocery store
and we will follow the map."
Sludge and I got up.
Our vacation was over.

I got two pieces of paper
and a pen.
I drew a map
on one piece of paper.

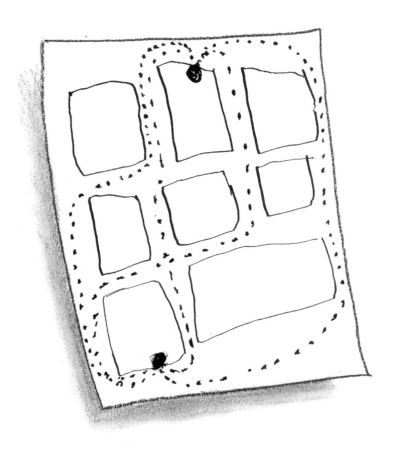

I wrote on the other:

Dear Mother,
Something is
lost. When I find
it, I will be back.
Love,
Nate the Great

Claude said,

"I will walk with you."

"Don't get lost," I said,

"or I will have

two cases to solve."

We walked between Claude's house

and the grocery store

and then between the grocery store

and Claude's house.

Sludge sniffed.

But we could not find the list.

"Perhaps it blew away," I said.

I dropped the map

on the ground.

"What are you doing?"

Claude asked.

"I am dropping the map.

Whichever direction it goes

will show us the way

the wind is blowing.

Perhaps your list blew

in the same direction."

The map blew toward Rosamond's
house and disappeared.
"I will go
to Rosamond's house," I said.
"I will ask her if
she has seen your list."

"I will go to my house
and wait," Claude said.
"We are in front
of your house," I said.
"Yes, that makes it
easy to find," Claude said.

Sludge and I went
to Rosamond's house.
Rosamond opened the door.
Rosamond is a very strange girl.
Today she looked
more than strange.
She looked strange and white.
She was covered with flour.
Sludge sniffed hard.
I sniffed hard.
Rosamond smelled terrific.
Pancakes!
She was making pancakes.
We walked in.
Rosamond's four black cats
were there.

Today they were white, too.

The cats looked at Sludge.

They were not afraid of him.

Nobody is afraid of Sludge.

"I am making cat pancakes

for my cats," Rosamond said,

"from a new recipe."

"I would like to taste

cat pancakes," I said.

"You are not a cat," Rosamond said.

"I would like to

taste them anyway," I said.

"A pancake is a pancake."

Rosamond and I sat down.

I ate a pancake.

It tasted fishy.

I ate another.

It tasted fishier.

"I am looking for Claude's
grocery list," I said.

"I think the wind blew it
toward your house.

Have you seen it?"

"I haven't seen a grocery list,"
Rosamond said. "But—"

"But what?"

"But I see Annie

and her dog, Fang,

outside my window, and—"

"And what?"

"And Fang has a piece of

paper in his mouth.

It might be the grocery list."

I got up.

"Thank you for your help

and your pancakes," I said.

"I am having a cat pancake party

this morning," Rosamond said.

"I have invited

all the cats I know.

Can you come?"

"I am not a cat," I said.

"That's what I told
you before," Rosamond said.
Sludge and I went out
to talk to Annie and Fang.
I like Annie.
I try to like Fang.
"Hello," I said. "I am looking
for Claude's grocery list,
and I think Fang has found it.

It's between his teeth."

"He won't let

that paper go," Annie said.

"Can you pull it out?" I asked.

"No," Annie said.

"Fang would get mad."

"I would not like to see

Fang mad," I said.

"I, Nate the Great, say

that we should keep anybody

with sharp teeth happy.

Very happy."

I had a problem.

How could I get the paper

out of Fang's mouth?

Suddenly I had the answer.

"Sludge," I said. "Bark!"

Sludge barked.

Sludge barks funny.

But that does not matter.

Fang barked back.

The piece of paper

dropped from his mouth.

I reached for it.

But the wind blew it
down the street.
I went after it.
Sludge went after me.
Fang went after Sludge.

Annie went after Fang.

The paper went around the corner.

I went around the corner.

Sludge went around the corner.

Fang went around the corner.

Annie went around the corner.

The paper blew

into a fence.

I grabbed the paper.

The case was almost over.

I looked at the paper.

I saw many lines.

The paper was my map.

"The list is still lost," I said.

"I need more clues."

I thanked Annie and Fang

for their help.

Sludge and I

walked to Claude's house.

Claude was home.

He was not lost.

It was a good sign.

"I, Nate the Great, have not

found your list," I said.

"Can you remember anything else

that was written on it?"

"How will that help

you find it?" Claude asked.

"Trust me," I said.

"I remember! I remember
two more things," Claude said.
"Eggs and baking powder."
"Very good," I said.
"Can you find the list
before lunch?" Claude asked.
"I hope so," I said.

"Come to my house at eleven."

Sludge and I walked home slowly.

This was a hard case. At home

I made myself some pancakes.

I mixed eggs, flour, salt,

baking powder, milk, butter,

and sugar together and cooked them.

I gave Sludge a bone.

I ate and thought.

I thought about the grocery list.

I thought about Rosamond

and her fishy cat pancakes.

I thought about Annie and Fang

and the map.

I put ideas together.

I took them apart.

Then I had a big idea.

I knew I must go back to

Rosamond's house.

I did not want to do that.

I did not want to be

at a party with Rosamond

and all the cats she knew.

But I had a job to do.

I had a case to solve.

Sludge and I walked quickly to

Rosamond's house.

I said hello to Rosamond

and more cats

than I could count.

They were all over

Rosamond's floor,

Rosamond's tables,

Rosamond's chairs,

and Rosamond.

"I came to talk about

your cat pancakes," I said.

"Would you like more?"

Rosamond asked.

"I would like to see

your recipe," I said.

"Here it is," Rosamond said.

"There are no directions

in this recipe," I said.

"I don't need any," Rosamond said.

"I just mix

some of everything together."

"Tell me, where did you

get this recipe?"

"I found it today," Rosamond said.

"Aha! You found it," I said.

"Did you find it

near your house?"

"Yes," Rosamond said.

"How did you know that?"

"I have something to tell you.

I, Nate the Great, say that
your cat pancake recipe
is Claude's grocery list."
I stood tall.
I cleared my throat.
I read the recipe.
"Salt
milk
butter
flour
tuna fish
eggs
baking powder
sugar
salmon
liver."

"Oh," Rosamond said.

"When I found the paper,

I thought it was a

cat pancake recipe."

"Yes," I said. "And when I
saw Fang holding a piece of paper,
I thought it was a grocery list.
I thought it was what I
hoped it was.

When you saw the grocery list,
you thought it was
what you hoped it was.
A cat pancake recipe.

I, Nate the Great, thought of that
when I was making pancakes.
I mixed eggs, flour, salt,
baking powder, milk, butter,
and sugar.
Claude had told me they
were on his list.
The other thing he remembered
on the list was tuna fish.
Cats like tuna fish.
So—cat pancakes!"

"Oh," Rosamond said.

"Well, Claude

can have his paper back.

I will keep the recipe

in my head."

"That is a good place for it,"

I said. "It cannot blow away."

I said good-bye to Rosamond

and more cats

than I could count.

Sludge and I went home

with the list.

The case was solved.

And it was almost eleven o'clock.

When Claude comes at eleven,

I will give him his list.

It is now past eleven o'clock.

It is now past eleven-thirty.

Claude has not shown up.

I do not see him anywhere.

I hope Claude has not lost

himself.

It is now past twelve.

Here comes Claude.

I am glad I do not have

to look for him.

I am glad the case is over.

I, Nate the Great,

have something important to do.

I, Nate the Great,

am going to finish

my vacation.

~Extra~
Fun Activities!

What's Inside

How did Claude lose his list?
The wind blew it away.
Nate wanted to know more.
He went to the library.
Here's what he found.

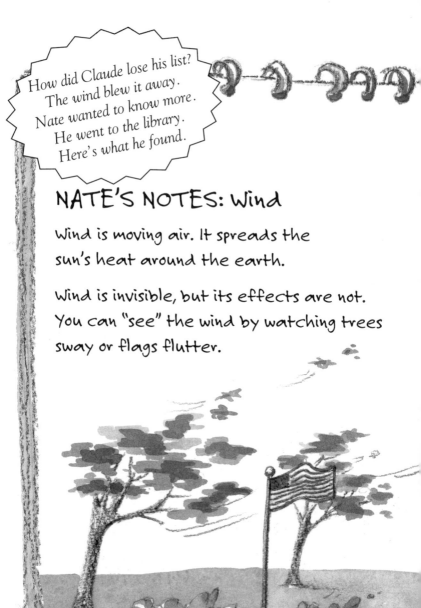

NATE'S NOTES: Wind

Wind is moving air. It spreads the sun's heat around the earth.

Wind is invisible, but its effects are not. You can "see" the wind by watching trees sway or flags flutter.

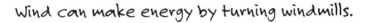

Wind can be gentle (a breeze).

Wind can be fierce (a hurricane).

Wind can make energy by turning windmills.

Winds as gentle as 13 miles per hour will "ground" mosquitoes. That means they can't fly. Bring on the wind!

How to Make a Pinwheel

*Pinwheels are fun! Make one and
learn more about how the wind works.*

Ask an adult to help you with this.

GET TOGETHER:

- a square piece of construction paper
- a new, unsharpened pencil with an eraser
- a ruler
- a straight pin
- scissors

MAKE YOUR PINWHEEL:

1. Lay the paper on a table. Use the pencil and the ruler to draw a line diagonally from each corner to the opposite one. When you're finished, the paper should look like this:

2. Use the pin to punch a small hole where the two lines cross.

3. Starting at the outer edge, cut along each line. Stop about an inch from the center hole. You can look at your ruler to see how long an inch is.

4. You now have four flaps. Use the pin to poke a hole in the top left corner of the top flap. Turn the paper so that a new flap is on top. Again, poke a hole in the top left corner. Repeat two more times, so that each flap has a hole in it.

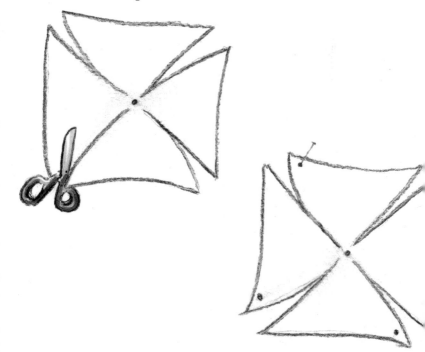

5. Pick up a flap at a punched corner. Carefully curl it toward the center hole. Slide the pin through the hole in the flap. Be sure not to poke yourself! Repeat with the other three flaps.

6. Now push the pin through the center hole. Your pinwheel should look like this one.

7. Lay the pencil on the table. Carefully push the pin into the eraser.

8. Hold the pinwheel by the pencil. Play with your pinwheel in the wind!

NATE'S NOTES: Maps

Nate likes maps. They're flat, easy to carry, and useful. He found some information about maps in the encyclopedia.

A MAP is a flat picture of all or part of the earth's surface. A GLOBE is a map drawn on a sphere (or ball). A CHART is a map used to navigate the ocean or another waterway.

A grid system makes a map easier to read. LONGITUDE lines run from north to south. LATITUDE lines run from east to west. The scale of a map shows how much smaller it is than the areas on the earth it depicts. An ARROW, or COMPASS, often shows you which way is north.

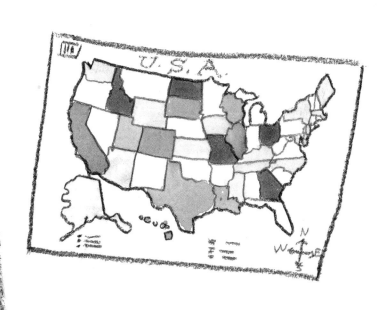

11

People also make globes and maps of the moon and the stars. It's harder to create a simple map of the sun, the moon, or the other planets because their positions change every day.

The oldest map in the world may be a small clay tablet about 4,000 years old. It shows part of a land called Mesopotamia. The area shown is now Iraq.

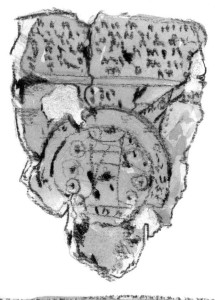

The first map of North America may be the " Vinland Map." Some experts date it to the year 1434. That's nearly sixty years before Columbus sailed to America. It probably shows part of what is now eastern Canada. Experts say Viking explorers drew the map. They called the area Vinland because of the grapevines they found growing there. Other experts consider this map a fake!

Google Earth is a really cool new kind of map. It lets you use your computer to "fly over" any location on earth. Get started at www.earth.google.com.

How to Make Cat Pancakes

Rosamond made pancakes for her cats to eat. Rosamond is weird. Pancakes are for people. If you really like cats, make these cat-shaped pancakes. But feed them to your friends, your family, and, of course, yourself.

Ask an adult to help you with this recipe.

GET TOGETHER:

- a mixing bowl
- 1 cup of flour
- a pinch of salt
- 2 tablespoons of sugar
- $1\frac{1}{2}$ teaspoons of baking powder
- 1 egg
- 2 tablespoons of melted butter
- $1\frac{1}{2}$ cups of milk
- a nonstick skillet
- cat-shaped cookie cutters
- syrup

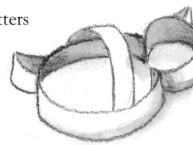

MAKE YOUR CAT PANCAKES:

1. In the bowl, mix together the flour, salt, sugar, and baking powder.
2. Add the egg, melted butter, and milk. Stir until just mixed together. Lumps are okay.
3. Warm the skillet over medium heat. Drop a tiny bit of water on the skillet. If the water skitters around, the skillet is hot enough.

4. For each pancake, pour about half a cup of batter onto the skillet. Wait until your pancakes have bubbles on top. Flip them. Cook them one more minute.
5. Put your pancakes on a plate. Use the cookie cutter to cut each pancake into one or more cat shapes.
6. Serve your pancakes with syrup on top.

Pancake trimmings make a good snack for a hungry dog.

Funny Pages

Q: What do cats eat for breakfast?
A: *Mice Krispies!*

Q: What do you call a cat who eats lemons?
A: *A sourpuss!*

Q: What do Italian cats like for dinner?
A: *Spa-catti!*

Q: What happened when the cat ate the comedian?
A: *He felt funny!*

Q: What does Rosamond feed her cats on a hot day?
A: *Mice cream cones!*

Q: What is Super Hex's favorite color?
A: *Purrple!*

How to Improve Your Memory

A detective needs a good memory. It helps the detective keep track of clues, or find the way home. Oliver could improve his memory with these tips. That is, if he could remember to use them.

Tip 1: *Pay attention to one thing at a time.* It's hard to remember anything if you are thinking about two things at once. That's why Nate usually takes only one case at a time!

Tip 2: *Get it right the first time.* "Unlearning" wrong information is more difficult than learning new information. So slow down and get your facts straight.

Tip 3: *Create a picture in your mind.*
To connect two facts you are trying to remember, make up a mental image. Make the picture silly if you can. Silly is easy to remember.

Say you are trying to remember that your cousin's birthday is November 10. You could imagine your cousin sitting down to Thanksgiving dinner—and eating ten turkeys! Thanksgiving helps you remember the month. The ten helps you recall the day.

Tip 4: *Create a story.*

Let's say you need to remember a short list, like a grocery list. Make up a story that aincludes all the items. Again, silliness works best. If your list includes salmon, red food coloring, and eggs, you might imagine a salmon swimming upstream to lay her eggs. But the salmon seems to be having a hard time. She pushes until she turns red in the face. Suddenly, out pops an egg! But it's not a salmon egg. It's a hen's egg! Test yourself. What were the three items on your list? That's right—salmon, red food coloring, and eggs.

Tip 5: *Use acrostics to remember how to spell words.* Take each letter of a hard-to-spell word. Assign a word to each one. Maybe you have a hard time remembering how to spell *beautiful.* See if it's easier to remember this phrase: "Beagles Eat Apples Under Tents IF U Leave."

Experts say cats have longer memories than dogs.
Cats can remember things for about 16 hours.
Dogs can only remember for about 5 minutes!

More Funny Pages

Doctor, Doctor, I've lost my memory!
When did this happen?
When did what happen?

Q: What did Annie's dog say to the vet who cured his memory loss?
A: *Fangs for the memories!*

Q: Why doesn't Claude have a
photographic memory?
A: *He doesn't have any film!*

a

Q: How are maps like fish?
A: *They both have scales!*

Q: Why don't maps ever win at cards?
A: *Because they always fold!*

Q: What game do people play at the grocery store?
A: *Price-tag!*

Q: What do bulls do when they go grocery shopping?
A: *They charge!*

Q: What color is the wind?
A: *Blew!*

Knock, knock.
Who's there?
Wendy.
Wendy who?
Wendy wind blows,
the cradle will rock.

Q: What did the book do
when a cold wind blew?
A: *Put on a book jacket!*

A word about learning with

Nate the Great

The Nate the Great series is good fun and has been entertaining children for over forty years. These books are also valuable learning tools in and out of the classroom.

Nate's world—his home, his friends, his neighborhood—is one that every young person recognizes. Nate introduces beginning readers and those who have graduated to early chapter books to the detective mystery genre, and they respond to Nate's commitment to solving the case and helping his friends.

What's more, as Nate the Great solves his cases, readers learn with him. Nate unravels mysteries by using evidence collection, cogent reasoning, problem-solving, analytical skills, and logic in a way that teaches readers to develop critical-thinking abilities. The stories help children start discussions about how to approach difficult situations and give them tools to resolve them.

When you read a Nate the Great book with a child, or when a child reads a Nate the Great mystery on his or her own, the child is guaranteed a satisfying ending that will have taught him or her important classroom and life skills. We know that you and your children will enjoy reading and learning from Nate the Great's wonderful stories as much as we do.

Find out more at NatetheGreatBooks.com.

Happy reading and learning with Nate!

Solve all the mysteries with

Nate the Great

- ❏ Nate the Great and the Crunchy Christmas
- ❏ Nate the Great Saves the King of Sweden
- ❏ Nate the Great and Me: The Case of the Fleeing Fang
- ❏ Nate the Great and the Monster Mess
- ❏ Nate the Great, San Francisco Detective
- ❏ Nate the Great and the Big Sniff
- ❏ Nate the Great on the Owl Express
- ❏ Nate the Great Talks Turkey
- ❏ Nate the Great and the Hungry Book Club
- ❏ Nate the Great, Where Are You?
- ❏ Nate the Great and the Missing Birthday Snake

MARJORIE WEINMAN SHARMAT has written more than 130 books for children and young adults, as well as movie and TV novelizations. Her books have been translated into twenty-four languages. The award-winning Nate the Great series, hailed in *Booklist* as "groundbreaking," has resulted in Nate's real-world appearances in many *New York Times* crossword puzzles, sporting a milk mustache in magazines and posters, residing on more than 28 million boxes of Cheerios, and touring the country in musical theater. Marjorie Weinman Sharmat and her husband, Mitchell Sharmat, have also coauthored many books, including titles in both the Nate the Great and the Olivia Sharp series.

MARC SIMONT won the Caldecott Medal for his artwork in *A Tree Is Nice* by Janice May Udry, as well as a Caldecott Honor for his own book, *The Stray Dog*. He illustrated the first twenty books in the Nate the Great series.